For Liberty

ORCHARD BOOKS
96 Leonard Street
London EC2A 4RH
Orchard Books Australia
14 Mars Road, Lane Cove, NSW 2066
ISBN 1 85213 542 5 (hardback)
ISBN 1 85213 848 3 (paperback)
First published in Great Britain 1993
First paperback publication 1995
© Nicola Smee 1993
The right of Nicola Smee to be identified as the author of this work
has been asserted by her in accordance with the
Copyright, Designs and Patents Act, 1988.
A CIP catalogue record for this book is available from the British Library.
Printed in Belgium

The Tusk Fairy

To Lizzie love Granny

Nicola Smee

ORCHARD BOOKS

Lizzie's favourite toy was her knitted
Elephant.

Granny had given him to Lizzie on the
day she was born, so they were exactly
the same age.

They had been through a lot together...

and over the years Elephant started to
look rather the worse for wear.

When Elephant's trunk started to unravel,
Lizzie bandaged it with some ribbon.

When his feet started to wear out and
stuffing poked through his knees...

Lizzie put her doll's socks on Elephant,
to keep everything in.

Then, when the wool on his back got
so thin you could see his insides, Lizzie
removed Teddy's trousers and put them
on Elephant to keep him all together.

Still, thread would occasionally appear
down the trouser legs.

Then one day a TERRIBLE thing happened!

Lizzie was giving her toys a ride when a thread from Elephant's ear got caught on a thorn.

By the time she noticed, all that was left of Elephant was – two tusks!

Lizzie followed the trail back, picking
up the trousers, the socks, bits of stuffing,
the ribbon and the unravelled wool.

Then she sat down with the remains and cried and cried and cried.

Granny ran out to see what had happened.

"Why don't you put the tusks under your pillow for the Tooth Fairy?" she said.

So that night, Lizzie put the tusks under her pillow and tried to sleep, while Granny hunted for some grey wool.

Eventually Lizzie fell into a deep dreamy sleep, so she didn't hear the sound of Granny's knitting needles clicking through the night.

"THE TUSK FAIRY'S BEEN! THE
TUSK FAIRY'S BEEN!"
Granny was woken by Lizzie's cries of delight.

Granny was tired but also delighted.
She had been worried when she found
she had run out of grey wool – but it
didn't seem to bother Lizzie.

And fond as they had been of 'Old' Elephant, the toys were pleased to see 'New' Elephant, as it meant they got their clothes back.

For the time being, anyway!